HANK THE COWDOG.

LET SLEEPING DOGS LIE

John R. Erickson 4/95

John R. Erickson

Illustrations by Gerald L. Holmes

Maverick Books
Published by Gulf Publishing Company
Houston, Texas

Maverick Books
Published by Gulf Publishing Company
P.O. Box 2608 Houston, Texas 77252-2608

10 9 8 7 6 5

Library of Congress Cataloging-in-Publication Data

Erickson, John R., 1943–
    Hank the Cowdog and let sleeping dogs lie.
    "The sixth exciting adventure in the
Hank the Cowdog series."
    Summary: Hank the Cowdog Head of
Ranch Security, pursues an elusive chicken
murderer.
    1. Dogs—Fiction. [1. Mystery and detective stories. 2. Dogs—Fiction. 3. Humorous stories. 4. West (U.S.)—Fiction]
I. Holmes, Gerald L., ill. II. Title. III. Title:
Let sleeping dogs lie.
[PS3555.R428H279 1988] 813'.54 [Fic]
88-29638
    ISBN 0-87719-139-5
    ISBN 0-87719-138-7 (pbk.)
    ISBN 0-87719-140-9 (cassette)

Printed in the United States of America

Cover design by Tom Hair

Contents

Chapter 1: An Awful Fiendish Murder..... 1

Chapter 2: The Case of the Moving Garden 13

Chapter 3: Another Triumph Over Pete.................................... 23

Chapter 4: Terminal Rootabegga and Another Murder.................... 37

Chapter 5: The Mailman Gets It............ 49

Chapter 6: An Unexpected Trip Into Spook Canyon............................. 59

Chapter 7: A Brilliant Interrogation of a Difficult Suspect.................. 69

Chapter 8: On Trial in the Horse Pasture..................................... 79

Chapter 9: Drover Confesses................. 89

Chapter 10: A New Twist in the Case.... 101

Chapter 11: The Sting Stings the Wrong Guy.................................... 113

Chapter 12: Breakfast is Cancelled......... 127

Have you read all of Hank's adventures?
Available in paperback at $6.95:

		Product #
1.	Hank the Cowdog	9130
2.	The Further Adventures of Hank the Cowdog	9117
3.	It's a Dog's Life	9128
4.	Murder in the Middle Pasture	9133
5.	Faded Love	9136
6.	Let Sleeping Dogs Lie	9138
7.	The Curse of the Incredible Priceless Corncob	9141
8.	The Case of the One-Eyed Killer Stud Horse	9144
9.	The Case of the Halloween Ghost	9147
10.	Every Dog Has His Day	9150
11.	Lost in the Dark Unchanted Forest	9118
12.	The Case of the Fiddle-Playing Fox	9170
13.	The Wounded Buzzard on Christmas Eve	9175
14.	Monkey Business	9180
15.	The Case of the Missing Cat	9185
16.	Lost in the Blinded Blizzard	9192
17.	The Case of the Car-Barkaholic Dog	9199
18.	The Case of the Hooking Bull	9212
19.	The Case of the Midnight Rustler	9218
20.	The Phantom in the Mirror	9232
21.	The Case of the Vampire Cat	9235
22.	The Case of the Double Bumblebee Sting	9246
23.	Moonlight Madness	9251

All books are available on audio cassette too!
($15.95 for two cassettes)

Also available on cassettes:
Hank the Cowdog's Greatest Hits!

Volume 1 Product #4120	$6.95
Volume 2 Product #4137	$6.95
Volume 3 Product #9194	$6.95

1

AN AWFUL FIENDISH MURDER

I t's me again, Hank the Cowdog. The night was dark and still, the air so heavy that I could taste it. And what I tasted was . . . *MURDER*!!

Drover had stumbled onto the body, what was left of it, down by the creek just before dark. He sounded the alarm and I raced to the scene. In the last light of day, I conducted my usual thorough investigation.

"Drover," I said after sifting the clues and analyzing the facts, "this was no ordinary murder. It's the work of some kind of fiend. And he may still be on the ranch."

"Oh my gosh! Maybe we better hide."

I caught him just as he was about to run for cover. "Hold on, son, I've got some bad news.

1

We're this ranch's first line of defense. If there's a murdering fiend on the loose, we have to catch him."

Drover shivered and rolled his eyes. "You're right about one thing."

"And what would that be, Drover?"

"It's bad news. I'm scared of murdering fiends."

"Being scared of scary things is normal, son. But you don't go into security work to be normal. We have to be tougher and braver than your ordinary run of mutts."

"Could I work on that tomorrow?"

"Negative. In this business, a guy never knows if he'll be around tomorrow."

"That's what I'm afraid of."

"Drover, being afraid is the major cause of fear. If you can get that under control, you've got it licked." He stared at me and then licked his chops. "When I said, 'You've got it licked,' I wasn't suggesting that you should lick your chops. Are you trying to be funny?"

"No."

"Good, because you're not."

"I'm too scared."

"Let's move out. We've got a job to do."

I sent Drover off to scout the eastern quadrant of headquarters while I gave myself the more difficult job of checking out the western quadrant, which included the saddle shed, corrals, calf shed, and feed barn.

As I groped through the inky blackness, I found myself worrying about Little Drover. What if he found the fiend? Or what if the fiend found him?

I crept through the front lot, sweeping the territory in front of me with eyes that had been trained to see what ordinary eyes were unable to see.

The wind stirred. No, the wind *moaned.* It moaned in the tops of the cottonwoods across the creek and cried through the pipes of the doctoring chute, and suddenly I heard a crash behind me. I leaped into the air and turned to face the attack of I-knew-not-what manner of monster . . .

. . . and realized that Slim and High Loper still hadn't taken the time to pound two piddling galvanized nails into that dadgum piece of tin on the roof of the calf shed.

Here we have a classic case of ranch mismanagement. How many years had that piece of tin flapped in the wind? Two? Five? Ten? Every time the wind changed directions, it banged. And every time it banged, Slim would say, "We'll have to fix that thing one of these days," and Loper would say, "Yup, when we get caught up."

And so it banged and flapped every time . . .

. . . THE WIND CHANGED DIRECTIONS.

There was my first clue. Yes, the pieces of the puzzle were beginning to fall into place. If

G.L. Holmes

the tin banged every time the wind changed direction, and if the tin was banging at that very moment, then it followed from simple deduction that *the wind had changed directions.*

Exactly what that had to do with the murder case, I wasn't sure, but I had a sneaking suspicion that the two were connected. The murderer was near. Somehow I had to get word to Drover.

The wind was rising now. Off to the north, a bolt of lightning cut through the night and bathed the caprock in ghostly silver light. Then came an ominous thumber of rundle . . . uh rumber of thundle . . . *rumble of thunder* while the tin banged against the roof of the calf shed.

Against the rising scream of the wind, I barked the retreat: "Drover, leave your post and come here at once!"

There was no reply but the mocking howl of the wind.

Dust and hay and flakes of dried manure swirled through the air, filling my eyes and mouth with dust and hay and flakes of dried manure that swirled through the air. Near blind and gasping for breath, I pitched forward.

Lightning crackled across the sky, and in the flash I saw something that froze the blood in my veins and raised the hair on my back.

There, standing some fifty feet in front of me, was a ghostly apparition—a glowing formless thing of pale light with deep blue holes where eyes should have been.

This was the fiend. It had to be.

Now, I'm no coward. I'll fight my weight in wildcats or skunks but I hate to mess with fiends. I needed help for this job, even if that meant exposing my position to the fiend. I raised my head and barked against the wind.

"Drover, can you hear me!"

Off in the distance, I heard a faint reply. "Yes! Can you hear me?"

"Affirmative!"

"What?"

"AFFIRMATIVE!"

"WHAT?"

"YES!"

"Oh." There was a throbbing silence. "What was the question?"

"The question was," I yelled against the wind, "can you hear me!"

"Oh. I thought that's what I asked you!"

"It was. Now listen carefully."

"Hank, can you hear me?"

"Of course I can hear you! That's what we've been yelling about."

"What? Hank, can you yell? I can't hear you."

"I haven't said anything yet, you dunce!"

"Oh. Well, tell me when you say something."

"Drover, listen carefully. I'm on patrol in the western quadrant. I've just made a visual sighting of an unidentified object. I think it's the fiend."

"Oh my gosh, I knew I should have stayed at the gas tanks, oh, my leg's killing me!"

"The important thing now, Drover, is not to panic."

"It's too late, I already did! Hank, I'm scared!"

"Get control of yourself. Give me your location."

"I don't know my location. I'm lost."

"How can you guard this ranch if you're lost?"

"What? I said, I'm lost! Help!"

"Hold your present location. I'm moving up to check this thing out. If you don't hear from me in an hour, run for the house and sound the alarm."

"I don't think I can find the house!"

"This will be a silent run, Drover. I'm breaking off communications as of this moment."

"Oh, my leg . . ."

I shifted into my Attack Mode, which is a kind of stealthy crouch I use only on Code 3's and Red Alerts. What it means is that I keep my body low to the ground while leading with my nose and following with a very stiff tail. In the Attack Mode I can cover short distances without making a sound.

If you've never seen a blue ribbon, top-of-the-line cowdog in Attack Mode, you'll just have to take my word for it. It's very impressive.

I crept forward as the lightning snapped overhead and the thumber rundled and the wind shrieked and the dust swirled. Up ahead, I could see the glowing thing lurking in the gloom.

Was I scared? Maybe. A little. After all, I'd never gone up against a fiend before. They're not very common.

Ten feet from the object, I stopped and took a deep breath. This was my last chance to back out, but as you might have already guessed, I didn't. I coiled my legs under me and sprang to the attack.

I struck the fiend with all my weight and

force and was a little surprised that he went down as easily as he did. I mean, I buried him, fellers, just by George bedded him down and jumped in the middle of him.

Suddenly, over the roar of the storm, I heard Drover. "Hank, help, Mayday, the fiend has me, help!"

G. L. Holmes

"There must be two of 'em, Drover! I've got my hands full here, so just fight for your life!"

My fiend began to fight back, which wasn't entirely unexpected. I hadn't supposed that I would win without a tussle. It seldom happens that way in real life. But the important thing is that I had the upper hand.

"I've got mine down, Drover! Give me a report on your situation."

"The fiend has me down, I'm whipped, I think I've lost a leg and a lot of blood, help, hurry, murder!"

"Hang on, Drover, I'll be right there!"

I hated to leave my fiend, just when I had him whipped, but a guy has to take care of his comrades. I stumbled off into the darkness, looking for Little Drover and hoping that I wasn't too late.

"Drover, can you hear me? Give me your position. The code word for this mission is Sea Cow."

"Help! Sea Cow! My leg!"

I groped toward the sound of his voice, and much to my surprise, I found him lying in the front lot. "Where is he, Drover, just point me toward him and stand back!"

"Oh, Hank, thank goodness you made it! I guess he ran away."

"Not a bad idea." I peered into the darkness. "He must have been a pretty smart fiend. Give me a damage report."

"Everything's damaged!"

The lightning was popping all around by this time and I was able to give Drover a quick check-up. "Son, I don't see a drop of blood and I count four legs and two ears. Are you sure you had a fight with a fiend?"

"I'm sure, Hank, it was a terrible fight, just terrible! He was about your size, only twice as big . . ."

"Hold it right there. If he was about my size, how could he have been twice as big?"

In a flash of lightning, I could see my assistant rolling his eyes around and twisting his mouth as he searched his tiny brain for the answer. "I guess he grew. Can a fiend do that?"

"Very possibly, Drover. As a matter of fact, mine was about *your* size when I jumped him, but he seemed to grow too. So there you are, some valuable information on the nature of fiends."

"Very valuable."

"And now you know what our next move will be."

"Sure do."

"And what will our next move be, Drover?"

"Well . . . go back to bed?"

I glared at the piece of darkness where his head had been only moments before. "No Drover, that's absolutely wrong." Lightning leaped across the sky and I saw that I was speaking to a fence post. Drover had moved.

"I'm over here now."

"Of course you are." I shifted around and faced him. "Our next move, Drover, will be to rush up to the house and sound the alarm. I think High Loper would like to know that he has a couple of fiends loose on this ranch."

And with that, we made a dash to the house. Little did I know that we would be exposing ourselves to danger of another sort.

C H A P T E R

2

THE CASE OF THE MOVING GARDEN

We went ripping out of the corral, me in the lead and Drover bringing up the rear. We zoomed past the saddle shed, under the front gate, and on an eastward course that would take us directly to the house. However, you might say that we never got there.

I knew something was wrong when I ran into a hogwire fence, hit that sucker dead center and put a pretty severe kink in my neck.

"Halt! Hold it right here! Unless I'm mistaken, someone has thrown up a hogwire fence. Obviously they don't want us to sound the alarm. The question is, *why*?"

"Yeah, but why?"

"I just asked that question."

"Oh."

13

"It wouldn't hurt, Drover, if you paid a little more attention to what's going on around here."

"Okay. You don't reckon we got into the garden by mistake, do you?"

"Impossible. The garden is a full fifteen degrees north of our present location. No, Drover, this is no garden. This is a new fence, thrown up by someone or something to keep us from warning the house. And you know what that means."

"Sure do."

"What?"

There was a long silence. "Well . . . it means that somebody around here knows how to dig postholes in the dark."

"Yes, but I'm talking about a deeper meaning."

"Oh."

"A meaning far darker and more sinister. It could mean, Drover, that this ranch is about to be attacked."

I heard him gasp. "By the fiends?"

"That's a possibility we can't ignore. Now the question is, how do we get past this barrier they've thrown into our path?"

I began pacing. My mind seems to work better when I pace. But it wasn't easy, pacing at this particular point in space, because the area was overgrown with weeds and noxious plants—a rather interesting clue, since this was around the first of May and weeds and noxious plants don't often appear so early in the Panhandle.

I salted that piece of information away for future reference and continued pacing. I could feel the weeds snapping beneath my feet. It takes a pretty stout variety of weed to keep me from pacing, especially when I'm putting clues together and following them to a logical conclusion.

"Drover, we have two contingency plans for a fence of this type: one, we go over it; two, we destroy it. Either way, it's nothing to sneeze at."

Drover sneezed.

I glared at him. "Why do you do things like that?"

"Like what?"

"When I say we've got this thing licked, you lick your chops. When I say this is nothing to sneeze at, you sneeze. Sometimes I think you're trying to make a mockery of my investigations."

"Doe. I'b allergic to domato plets."

"That's all?"

"Cross by hard and hobe to die." He crossed his heart.

"All right. Then the question we have to

G.L. Holmes

face now is—if you're allergic to tomato plants, why are these *weeds* making you sneeze? Until we answer that question . . .''

Suddenly I froze. My nose shot up, just as a bolt of lightning struck one of the cottonwoods down by the creek. The flash was followed by a loud boom.

"Wait a minute, I think I've got it!"

"Oh-h-h, I think I got it too!" Drover was lying on the ground with his paws over his eyes.

"Get up, Drover. This case is taking on an entirely new dimension. Sniff the air and tell me what you smell."

"Okay." He pushed himself up and sniffed that air. "I sbell domato plets." He sneezed.

"Exactly! And where does one usually find tomato plants?"

"Uh . . . in a garden?"

"Exactly! Our clues are falling into place. Follow them to the logical answer."

"Okay. The answer is . . . yes."

"No."

"Doesn't it have to be one or the other?"

"Yes and no."

"Oh, okay."

"In most instances, a simple yes or no will do, but in this particular case the answer is more complicated, for you see, Drover, we have stumbled into *a garden*."

"Isn't that what I said a while ago?"

"You were close, very close considering your limited, uh, gifts. You did in fact suggest that we had stumbled into the garden by mistake."

"I thought that's what I said."

"But what you didn't take into account, Drover, was that *the entire garden had been moved fifteen degrees to the south!*"

"No fooling?"

"Yes. We have walked into a trap."

"Uh oh."

"The purpose of which was to keep us from sounding the alarm. But what they didn't take into account was our superior barking ability."

"You mean . . ."

"Exactly. We may be cut off from the house, Drover, but we can still sound the alarm. On the count of three, we'll commence barking. One! And I want you to put your heart and soul into it. Two! Just by George bark as you've never barked in all your life. Three!"

"Now?"

"Let 'er rip!"

Fellers, we leaned into the task and did some heavy duty barking. Drover did his usual "yip-

yip-yip, pause, yip-yip-yip, pause, yip-yip-yip, etc.'' And on each yip, all four of his feet left the ground. Funny how he does that.

"I added my deep masculine roar, the same brand of barking that has struck terror in the hearts of monsters, coyotes, coons, badgers, skunks, rattlesnakes, and cats—not to mention cattle, which are my specialty.

Loper wasn't what you would call swift in responding to our call. It took us a good fifteen minutes of solid barking to get a light on in the house. At last we heard his voice:

"SHUT UP, YOU IDIOTS!!''

We kept it up, just barked our hearts out. Suddenly we saw a flash of light, followed by a boom and a sprinkling of buckshot in the trees.

Drover stopped barking. "Is he shooting at us?''

I gave him a withering glare. "How dumb do you think he is? He must have seen one of the fiends. Keep barking and maybe we can get him down here.''

We sent up another salvo of high explosive barking. Before long, I saw the beam of a flashlight and heard the yard gate slam. At last we were getting somewhere.

"Keep it up, Drover. We want to give him

our coordinates. Otherwise, he'll never hear us with all this thunder."

We kept up a steady barrage. The flashlight came closer, then pieces of Loper began to take shape in the darkness: cowboy boots, skinny white legs, striped boxer shorts, white

G. L. Holmes

belly, hairy chest, angry face, cowboy hat, shotgun.

He hadn't bothered to dress up, but that was okay. What mattered was that he was there with his gun.

He leaned on the fence and threw his light around the garden. It revealed a, shall we say, dismal scene of tomato plants, radishes, lettuce, turnips, and other young vegetables tromped flat on the ground by unknown forces.

Then I heard Loper's voice. "Holy smokes, my wife is gonna kill somebody! The coons must have . . ."

The light hit me, punched me right in the retinas, kind of hurt. I squinted but held my head up high and gave my tail such a big sweeping wag that I got a piece of tomato plant caught in them long hairs out near the end, had to reach back and pull if off with my teeth.

It was still hanging from my mouth when I heard Loper say, "Oh no, I don't believe this. Hank, you idiot, you nincompoop, you moron!"

HUH? I glanced at Drover. He had disappeared.

"You pea-brained, manure-headed, sewer-dipping, ignert, garden-destroying, barking-all-night, sorry excuse for a cowdog, GET YOUR TAIL OUT OF SALLY MAY'S GARDEN!!!!''

What . . . how . . . but   I . . . now   hold on . . .

I heard him pump a shell into the chamber and figgered the time had come for me to sell out, never mind the explanations. I made a dive out of the flashlight beam and took aim for the feed barn.

Just then the rain hit, and I'm talking about hard rain, fellers, big drops and plenty of them, buckets of water, raining down snakes and weasles and pitchforks. I made it to the feed barn just in time, slithered through that place at the bottom where the door's warped, and crawled inside.

In other words, I escaped serious wetting by a matter of seconds.

That's the good part of the story. The unfortunate part is that Loper and his shotgun, shall we say, didn't escape serious wetting.

They got drenched, soaked. But that wasn't my fault.

3

ANOTHER TRIUMPH
OVER PETE

Drover showed up around 8:00 the next morning. By that time I'd already been up for a couple of hours, going over the scene of last night's investigation—in heavy mud, I might add. Mud has never yet scared me off a case.

I caught sight of him out of the corner of my eye, padding down the hill from the machine shed, where, no doubt, he had spent a dry comfortable night curled up in the northwest corner beside Loper's canoe, while I had tossed and turned and dreamed about the un-solved murder.

He came skipping down the hill with his eyes going back and forth to the trees, the clouds, the butterflies, and other silly things. I mean, you would have thought the little runt didn't have a care in the world. And maybe he didn't. That seems to be one advantage of below-average intelligence.

But I had plenty of cares in the world—namely last night's wreck in the garden, which I had just about solved, and a murder case, which I just about hadn't solved.

I had been studying The Case of the Moving Garden since daylight, and it was very much on my mind when Mister Look-At-The-Butterflies finally put in his appearance.

"Hi Hank. Sure is a pretty day."

"That's a matter of opinion. Get over here. I've got things to discuss with you."

"Oh good."

"You won't think 'oh good' when you hear 'em."

"Oh rats."

He came over to the corner of the saddle shed where I was standing. "Sit down." He sat down and gave me his patented Drover Look: two eyes, clear and wide, that revealed absolutely nothing behind them. "I've been going over this case."

"Which case?"

I studied him. "What do you mean, which

case? Do you remember anything that happened last night?"

He twisted his mouth and squinted one eye. "Well, let's see. I heard a mouse in the machine shed . . . and it rained, boy we had a terrible storm up at the machine shed."

"What about fighting with the fiends? What about being trapped in the garden?"

"Oh yeah."

"And what about your disappearing act when Loper showed up with the flashlight? You remember any of that?"

"It's kind of hazy."

"And the trampled tomato plants?"

He sneezed. "It's coming back now. They bade be sdeeze."

"Very good, Drover. Now I want you to listen. I've been working the case this morning and I think I've got it solved."

"Oh good."

I marched back and forth in front of him, softened my voice, and gave him a disarming smile. "But I need to ask you a question or two."

"Sure, Hank, ask me anything."

"All rightsie. Now, if you recall, your orders last night were to patrol the eastern quadrant of headquarters, yet after our tussle with a pair of fiends, you turned up in the middle of the front lot, which is in the *western* quadrant of headquarters. Could you explain how that happened?"

"Well . . . it was awful dark and . . . maybe I got lost."

"I see. Maybe you got lost. Is it possible, Drover, that you never made it to your alleged territory? Is it possible that you were in the front lot all the time?"

"Well . . ."

"Is it possible that I was foolish enough to believe you were in your assigned territory and mistook you for a fiend?"

"That's an interesting question."

"Yes indeed. And here's another one: is it possible that, instead of scuffling with a pair of fiends, you and I were scuffling with each other?"

"Well . . ."

Suddenly I whirled around. "You needn't answer because I'm telling you that's what happened. There were no fiends, Drover, only your mutton-headed incompetence. And if there were no fiends, then it follows that fiends couldn't have moved the garden fifteen degrees to the south."

"I guess not."

"Look at that garden. Does it appear to you that it's been moved in the last 24 hours?"

He squinted his eyes. "Well . . ."

"Of course it hasn't been moved! What kind of moron would think a garden could be moved?"

"Well . . . it sounded okay last night."

"To you maybe, but I smelled a rat from the very beginning. I never quite swallowed that story, but guess who got caught admidst the trampled vegetables. And blamed."

There was a long silence as Drover studied the clouds. "Well let's see . . ."

"I got the blame, as usual. Do you understand the position you've put me in?"

His head began to sink.

"You've made me look like a complete fool. My reputation has suffered irrepressible harm, all because you didn't go where you were assigned to go—and also because you're a sawed-off, chicken-hearted little dunce."

A tear rolled down his face. "I don't mean to be."

"I ought to strip you of your rank."

"I don't have any rank."

"Oh yes you do. As of this moment, I'm promoting you to First Deputy Assistant Head of Ranch Security."

"Thanks, Hank."

"Congratulations. And as of this moment, I'm stripping you of your rank. You're busted, Drover, you're back where you started, and I'm afraid this will have to go in your dossier."

"Oh darn."

"And one last thing. The next time we get caught in some act of foolishness, would you please not disappear and run to the machine shed?"

"Well . . . wouldn't it make me look bad if I got caught?"

"Yes, it would, Drover, but that's the whole point. I would like to share the blame with you."

"That's mighty thoughtful."

"It's the least I can do. I mean, a guy can't go around thinking of himself all the time."

"Yeah, 'cause if he does, he never thinks of anyone but himself."

"Right. He becomes self-centered and callous. He cuts himself off from the, the, the warmth and communion of other creatures."

"And in the wintertime, that can be mighty cold."

"Exactly. Sharing is what this life is all about, Drover. And that's why I want you to go sit in the garden this morning."

"All morning?"

"Just until Sally May comes down."

"Well . . . what if she thinks I tore up the tomato plants?"

I studied the sky. "That's a risk you'll have to take, but I think the experience will be worth it. Just remember that this is a sharing experience."

"A sharing experience."

I put my paw on his shoulder. "I want to do this for you, Drover. I think it's important to your growth and education."

"Well . . . if you really think . . ."

"I do. Now scram, go sit in the garden."

"I'm liable to start sneezing."

"That's fine, no problem. If you feel a sneeze coming on, just rear back and by George express yourself. That's one of your problems, Drover, you don't express yourself enough."

"Well, okay. Just sit in the garden, huh?"

"Right. And think of sharing."

"Okay, Hank, here I go." And off he went, skipping into the garden. As per my orders, he sat down in the midst of the wreckage and started sneezing.

You might say that I slipped around the

corner and took cover behind the saddle shed, since I didn't want to, uh, hog all the attention. I figgered Sally May would be down in 10–15 minutes to survey the damage, and then the fireworks would start.

My conscience bothered me for a solid minute and a half. I mean, it takes a certain kind of vision and toughness for a guy to send his men out on a suicide mission, even when he knows in his heart it's for their own good. But as they say, "If you can't stand the heat, don't sleep in the oven."

The minutes dragged by, first five minutes, then ten, then fifteen, in that order. Sally May didn't show. I was getting bored and restless. I had many things to do on my list of things to do. I ain't the kind of dog who's content to sit around counting the flies, regardless of how many flies there are.

I peeked around the corner of the saddle shed, and what I saw may come as a surprise. I saw, not Sally May, as you might have suspected, for she was nowhere to be seen; but Pete the Barncat—a local character for whom I had very little use.

It would have been very satisfying to me personally, as one of Pete's more devoted enemies, if Sally May had appeared at that moment, for she just might have leaped to the conclusion that her treasured cat had contributed to the damage.

I couldn't help smiling. My plan was working to perfection, for you see, it had been part of my plan that Pete would come along, step into the trap I had so carefully laid for him, and get himself showered with rocks and clods by an outraged Sally May.

Your average barncat is no match for a highly conditioned, highly trained, thoroughly disciplined cowdog with a mastery of battlefield strategy and the, shall we say, nasty little twists of a well planned espionage operation.

Yes. It was all going according to plan. Very shortly, Sally May would appear and Pete would become *kitty non grata,* which was only fair and right because Pete was about as non grata as any cat I'd ever come across.

Sally May didn't show. The minutes ticked by and I found myself observing Drover and the cat. It suddenly occurred to me that something odd was going on between them.

Clue #1: Instead of talking in a normal voice, they began to whisper.

Clue #2: They were casting glances in my direction.

Clue #3: Upon completion of #1 and #2,

they went into periods of extended laughter.

In security work, it's an established rule that it takes three clues to make a case. One clue might be the result of coincidence. Two clues should arouse suspicion. Three clues should be followed up with further investigation.

And I was just the guy who could handle that little situation. I swaggered out, ducked under the wooden gate there beside the saddle shed, and marched my bad self over to the garden.

G.L. Holmes

Pete had been whispering in Drover's ear. When he saw my enormous hulk looming up before him, he ceased his whispering and giggling and other forms of silly behavior and said, "Hmm, my goodness, the cops are here."

"You got that right, son. Now, I'm very busy and I want some straight answers. Number one, what's going on around here—and don't bother to lie because I've had you under surveillance for the last hour."

Drover spoke up. "We were just talking."

"That's right, Hankie, we were just . . . talking."

"I'm well aware that you were talking, cat, and I have reason to think you were talking about ME."

Pete arched his back and started digging his claws into the dirt. "Why would we want to talk about such a boring subject?"

"Out with it, cat. What were you saying?"

"Well," said Pete, "I just bet Drover a chicken bone that if we looked toward the saddle shed and laughed, you'd be in the garden within thirty seconds."

Drover nodded his head. "That's what he said, all right."

"That's just what I thought he said," I said.

"And then," Drover went on, "he bet me

another chicken bone that when you got here, you wouldn't close your eyes, turn around three times, and count to twenty.''

''Oh yeah?'' I shot a wicked grin at the cat. ''You were foolish enough to bet against me on that, huh? Well, I've got some bad news, Kitty-Kitty. You just lost the bet.''

Pete yawned and flicked the end of his tail. ''You haven't done it yet.''

I went nose-to-nose with him. ''No, but I'm fixing to. The next time you want to outsmart Hank the Cowdog, you'd better bring your lunch, because it's liable to take you all day.''

Pete grinned. ''I still don't think you'll do it.''

''Oh yeah? Stand back and study your lessons.''

They moved back and gave me some room and I began the maneuver. I closed my eyes, turned around twenty times, and counted to three.

In the midst of this procedure, I found myself wondering why Pete had issued such a silly challenge. I mean, this was a piece of cake for me. But I had learned long ago not to apply logic to the behavior of a cat.

''There we are, and you lose the bet.'' I opened my eyes, staggered five steps to the north (you might say that those twenty turn-arounds left me a little dizzy), and noticed . . .

HUH?

Pete and Drover had vanished.

Sally May and Little Alfred, her three-year-old son, were standing on the other side of the

G.L. Holmes

hogwire fence. Her hair was up in curlers, her eyes were up in flames, and she was reaching for a clod.

"YOU'VE RUINED MY GARDEN, YOU NASTY DOG!!"

Hey, wait a minute . . . there was a simple explanation . . .

Sally May had a good arm and a deadly aim. The clod got me in the ribs on the left side. I lit a shuck and got the heck out of there.

In some respects, the confrontation with Sally May turned out to be a, shall we say, negative experience for me personally. Yes, I took a few lumps. But throbbing ribs and a tongue-lashing were a small price to pay for a triumph on the strategic side of the ledger.

For once again, I had beat Pete the Barncat at his own shabby game.

CHAPTER

4

TERMINAL ROOTABEGGA AND ANOTHER MURDER

Well, in just a few short hours I had knocked out several pieces of work. Not only had I notched up a moral victory over Pete, but I had solved The Case of the Moving Garden.

Your ordinary run of ranch dog would have gone back to bed, figgering he had already put in a day's work. But me? No sir. Even though I had stayed up half the night sifting clues, it never occurred to me to go back to bed.

All right, maybe it occurred to me, but iron discipline prevailed.

I laid low in the sick pen while Sally May rumbled over her tomato plants and tried to keep Little Alfred from wandering down to the creek. When I heard the slap-slap of rubber thongs against her feet, I peeked out and saw her walking back to the house. The coast was clear and I made a dash for the sewer.

This was the spot where the septic tank overflowed, don't you see. It held the magic green waters that healed the sick and impressed the women. Not that I was particularly sick or planning to sweep any women off their feet, but while we're on the subject of women, it had been a while since I had seen the lovely Miss Beulah.

Oh, be still, my heart! She had visited my gunny sack many times at night, a scented phantom in my dreams that troubled my sleep and left me calling her name in the darkness. Couldn't get that woman off my mind. Why she wasted her time with Plato the Bird Dog, I just didn't know. Imagine the torment that must have caused her!

Anyway, where was I? Sewer. A regular course of mineral baths was part of my overall fitness program, and I tried not to think of Beulah during working hours.

I climbed out of the sewer, gave myself a good shake, and headed down to the creek to study the scene of the murder one more time. That case had me stumped. I had reached a dead end. I hoped I might find some little piece of evidence I had missed the first time.

If I had found a new piece of evidence, it would have been *little*. There just wasn't much left of the victim—maybe a double handful of feathers, four of five toenails, and a beak.

I tried to put the clues into a pattern and build a profile of the murderer. He had a taste for young, plump chickens but obviously he didn't care for beaks, toenails, or feathers.

Hmmmm. Not much of a profile there. That description fit a wide range of characters, including, well . . . me. I was no fiend, you understand, but no fool either. In the unlikely event that I had decided to break the law and eat a young, plump chicken, I would have devoured everything but toenails, feathers, and the beak.

There's no chance that I would have risked my career for the momentary delight of eating a young, plump, tender, juicy chicken. But if I had, and I repeat, this is strictly a hypogorical example, I would have left the aforementioned parts.

So I was back to Point Zero. I checked for tracks but found only mine and Drover's and a few smudged prints that I couldn't identify.

Maybe the killer had smudged feet. Then again, maybe he didn't.

I was deep in thought, following each lead until it vanished into thin air, when something strange occurred. I sort of passed out, fainted. Nothing like that had ever happened to me before. One minute I was sitting there beside the creek, and the next thing I knew, I woke up near some willows, maybe fifty feet downstream.

Kind of scared me, to be honest about it. I knew I'd been working hard, staying up late at night, burning the flashlight at both ends, you might say, but I hadn't realized that it had taken such a toll on my body.

I mean, to some of us overwork is just a normal condition. You get used to a grinding schedule, sacrificing everything for the ranch, giving up your private life for something you believe in, and you just don't notice that it's chipping away at your physical and psycho-mechanical whatever.

This is especially true, I might point out, when a guy starts out with a rather magnificent array of physical gifts: eyes that see in the dark, ears that can hear a prairie dog in its hole, a heart that pumps blood twenty-four hours a day, rain or shine, and finally, an overall body that causes monsters to shrink in fear and women to faint.

But what a guy tends to forget is the joker in the deck of life: time. Time not only marches on, it marches right over the top of a guy, steps on his nose and tail and leaves boot prints up and down his back.

Maybe the years were catching up with me. Maybe I'd been pushing myself too hard. Maybe all the cares and worries of running the ranch had begun to grind me down. Maybe I had hardening of the asteroids or high blood pressure or low blood pressure or terminal rootabegga.

I had seen other dogs go down with those afflictions. Maybe it was my turn. Maybe, after a long and glorious career in security work, I had finally burned myself out.

I was in the midst of these depressing thoughts when Drover came streaking down from the corrals. He was yip-yip-yipping and obviously in a state of excitement, if not sheer panic.

"Hank, oh Hank, they're back, come quick, Mayday, help, blood, murder!"

There are no holidays at the top. I pushed myself up to face the latest crisis on the ranch. Drover was there in front of me, jumping up and down and squeaking. "Drover, please don't squeak."

"Okay, Hank, but . . ."

"And quit hopping up and down. Hold still, try to get control of yourself." He quit hopping and squeaking, which helped a bunch. "Now, I don't expect you to care that I'm showing early symptoms of terminal rootabegga, but you might as well know about it now."

"What is it?"

"It's a rare and dreaded disease. One minute you feel great; the next, bingo, you're down, with one foot in the grave."

"Well, that still leaves you with three."

I gave him my most patient glare. "That's true, Drover, and I'm touched by your concern. It's times like these that make a guy appreciate all the wonderful friends he doesn't have."

"That's what friends are for."

"Yes, I know, and what I wouldn't give to have just one!"

"Oh, you've won plenty, Hank, but you can't win 'em all."

"That may be the smartest thing you ever said, Drover."

"Thanks."

"And it's complete nonsense. Now, tell me

why you came down here—slowly, calmly, without your usual hysterics."

His eyes blanked out. "Let's see, why *did* I come down here?"

"You were excited about something. You were yipping and hopping."

He shook his head. "Must have been pretty important."

"Are you telling me you've forgotten?"

"Heck no. You might get mad."

"Something about blood."

"Blood?"

"And murder."

"Murder? Sounds awful. Sure wish I could . . . oh Hank, blood and murder, they're back on the ranch!"

I poked him in the chest with my paw. "*Who's* back on the ranch? Spit it out, you're burning daylight."

"The killers! They struck again, in broad daylight!"

"HUH? You mean, there's been another murder?"

"Yes! Oh, it's awful and I'm scared."

Well, that bit of news sent a shock clean out to the end of my tail. Never mind that I was on death's front porch, I had to get cracking again and protect the ranch.

I went streaking up the hill. "Come on, Drover, follow me!"

"Do you know where you're going?"

I stopped and waited for him to catch up. "Drover, you neglected to mention one small piece of information. Where are we going?"

"Well, let's see . . . you know, I can't remember."

"Oh for crying out loud!"

"Wait a minute, wait a minute, I've got it! Behind the machine shed."

We went tearing up the hill, me in the lead and Drover bringing up the rear. In the middle of those dead weeds behind the machine shed, five paces east of the one-way plow, I found the evidence. And I was astonished at how little evidence there was. Nothing but three white feathers!

"Holy cats, Drover, the killers not only ate all the meat and bones this time, they ate the beak and toenails and most of the feathers. And there's no blood whatsoever."

He came up and looked at the scene. "Kind of scary, ain't it?"

"It certainly is, but I'm beginning to see a pattern in these killings."

He nodded his head. "Yeah, and there's an

even better pattern over here where the chicken got killed."

"Huh?"

He moved six paces to the east and stood over a familiar sight: a double-handful of

G.L.Holmes

feathers, toenails, a beak, and blood stains in the dirt.

I joined him. "Yes, I see what you mean. This pattern is better. And what's more important, it matches the M.O. of last night's killing." I started pawing up dirt and throwing it on the feathers, etc.

"Hey, be careful, you're covering up the evidence."

I finished the job and turned to Drover. "Of course I was covering the evidence. And I suppose I have to explain why."

"Might be a good idea."

"Very well, listen carefully." I tossed a glance over both shoulders and lowered my voice. "We have studied the evidence and found a pattern, right? What's to keep the killer from coming back, studying the same evidence, and discovering the same pattern? And then using it? Had you thought of that?"

"Not really."

"Well, there you are. We can't allow our evidence to be used to encourage criminal behavior, and furthermore, if Loper and Sally May find out they've lost two pullets in two days, they're liable to think we're not doing our job."

"Never thought of that."

"Which might contain a germ of truth, and I don't need to tell you how dangerous germs can be." Drover is so predictable. He sneezed. "There, you see? Through a process of simple deduction, we've proved my original point. For now, the best thing we can do is forget we ever saw this evidence and try to build up our resistance to germs."

And with that, I put The Case of the Vanishing Chickens on temporary hold.

CHAPTER

5

THE MAILMAN GETS IT

We left the murder scene and moved around to the front of the machine shed. Drover went straight to the upside-down Ford hubcap which serves as our food bowl and started crunching the latest offering of Co-op dog food.

Funny, I wasn't at all hungry, even though I couldn't remember the last time I'd eaten. Should have been hungry. I went over and sniffed the grub. It just didn't excite me. Maybe I was getting tired of Co-op.

At that moment my ears shot up. I heard a vehicle coming down the county road and suddenly I had a terrible thought: we had gotten so bogged down in cases and investigations, we had let the mailman go four or five days without a good barking.

Now I'm well aware that in the world of murders and so forth, easing up on the mailman might not sound like a catastrophe. But let me tell you something about these post office people. If you let 'em go too long without a good stiff challenge, they start getting some funny ideas.

My Uncle Beanie, one of the all-time greats at mail truck barking, used to say that the first thing he did every morning was to ask himself the question, "Whose ranch is this?" He claimed that a cowdog's first job is to clear up the matter of ownership.

Your cocker spaniels and your poodles and your other inferior breeds might not care whose ranch it is, but it's priority number one for us cowdogs. It's OUR ranch, period. We try to be big about it. We try not to rub it in. We try not to become overbearing. But there's a limit to how nice you can be in saying, THIS IS MY RANCH.

I mean, as long as everyone respects our country, we get along fine. We don't mind people looking, don't you know, but if they drive or walk or fly across our country, we want to know the reason why.

And post office people are notorious for driving up and down the roads without permission. They'll sneak onto the ranch, slip up to the mailbox, make some suspicious movements which no one has ever bothered to explain to me, and then hurry away.

Why are they so sneaky? What are they actually doing in that mail box? And why do they drive away in such a hurry? Until a dog gets a few answers to these questions, he can't afford to take any chances with the mailman.

"Drover, I'm going up to intercept the mailman. Can you hold things down here until I get back?"

He was still crunching his Co-op. Sounded like he was eating rocks. He nodded his head and gave me a silly grin. "Sure, Hank. Don't worry about a thing."

"All right, and don't talk with your mouth full. You just spit some crumbs on me. I should be back within half an hour."

He nodded and waved goodbye. And with that, I swaggered out to intercept the mailman, singing the cowdog song for the occasion, "Bark At The Mailman Battle Hymn." (The tune is the same as "God Of Our Father," if you'd care to sing along). To do the song properly, you need a full orchestra and chorus in the background, but that isn't always possible under pasture conditions.

Bark At The Mailman Battle Hymn

Bark at the mailman, give him the full load.
He has no business driving on my road.
I am in charge of Ranch Security.
Trespassers must have permits cleared by me.

Postal employees just don't understand
Dangers they risk when slipping on my land.
What are you doing at my mailbox, sire?
Get off my ranch or I shall bite your tires!

Pretty good song, huh? You won't find too many songs that will inspire a cowdog more than "Bark At The Mailman Battle Hymn." After a couple of verses, I'm ready to go out and by George do some damage.

I loped out into the pasture and watched the approach of the trespasser. He crossed the bridge there at Spook Canyon and rattled over the cattle guard between the horse pasture and the home pasture. He had entered Security Zone Alpha (that's sort of a code name we use for the home pasture) and I couldn't be held responsible for anything that followed.

I went into my combat configuration. First, I stretched out flat on the ground, giving myself such a low profile that I became almost invisible. Second, I pinned back my ears. Third, I stiffened my tail to its full-alert position. Fourth, I initiated my Growling Mode. Fifth and finally, I unsheathed my fangs, which is something I can do by tensing the *monosodium pectorus* muscles in my cheeks.

(Don't bother to memorize these technical terms. Unless you're involved in security work on a daily basis, you won't have much call for them).

As the pickup pulled off the road and bounced to a stop beside the mailbox, I began creeping forward. By the time the mailman had lowered the flag on the box and snapped the door shut, I was up on my feet, gliding across the pasture. The instant I saw the pickup pull away, I hit full throttle.

G.L. Holmes

And fellers, the attack was on! First I barked the tail pipe and the right rear tire. Then I zoomed around and barked the left rear tire. Then I executed a very tricky maneuver which most dogs won't even attempt. Running at full tilt, I swooped in and *bit* the left front tire!

And I should point out that I did this in full view of the mailman—a big, tall, ugly guy who had lost most of the hair on top of his head but wore a Farm Bureau cap to cover it. And did I mention the tumor on his left cheek? Had a big tumor on his left cheek, some kind of deformity that made him look extra mean.

Most dogs would have been scared. Me? No sir. The way I look at it, the bigger the mailman, the slower the truck. Glancing up as I dived at the tire, I could see lines of fear etched on his face. By then he must have known the extent of his peril.

I mean, let's face the brutal fact. On a good run, when conditions are just right, I can tear the tread off a steel-belted radial tire, just bust it like a child's balloon. And on a few rare occasions, I've been known to tear the wheel off the . . . whatever it is the wheel is bolted to, axle I guess, shearing off lug bolts as though they were toothpicks.

So who could blame the mailman for showing fear? Terror is the proper response to the terrible. He made the only sensible decision under the circumstances: he cobbed that pickup and went roaring away.

It was a nice move, made just in the nick of time. I had been unable to sink my teeth into his tire or get the kind of penetration I needed to cause a blowout, so he escaped pretty muchly unharmed. Another thirty seconds and . . . well, he lucked out this time.

On your short sprints and your lightning dashes, I can equal or beat any breed of pickup, but on your longer hauls they can wear me down after, oh, two-three hundred yards. The mailman pulled away from me, but I barked him all the way to the next cattle guard. And just to be on the safe side, I stood in the middle of the road for another five minutes, waiting to see if he dared come back.

He didn't. My guess is that he lit a shuck back to the post office, turned in his uniform, and went looking for a safer job.

By the way, I solved the Case of the Left Cheek Tumor. Turned out to be chewing tobacco. I know, because before he left he spit at me (he missed). Also yelled something about an "ignert sunny bridge." Exactly what he meant by that I wasn't sure, but I didn't care for his tone of voice, and I made a mental note not to let him off so easy next time.

Well, that was a nice piece of ranch work, the kind of job-well-done that makes a dog feel a little glow of pride. I was making my way back to headquarters, walking down the center of the road (it was my road, after all, and I figgered I might as well use the whole son of a gun), when I heard the sound of a motor in the distance.

At first I thought it might be the mailman streaking back to town to turn in his mail sack, but at a glance I could see that it wasn't. This was a different vehicle.

Hmmmm. I sat down in the road and studied on it. For the past six months I'd noticed an increase in oil field traffic on my road: pumpers, company men, trucks. These were all unauthorized vehicles. I'd been letting them cross without permission because, well, put a pencil to it.

How far can you spread a dog, even a good one? My case load had been so heavy over the past year that I'd hardly had time even to monitor the mail truck. Keeping up with oil field traffic was just more than I could handle. I couldn't do a good job working murder cases and traffic too.

You'd think I might have gotten some help from Drover, but I'd never been satisfied with his performance. Several times I'd pulled him off traffic entirely after I'd caught him sitting in the ditch and watching trucks go by.

Anyway, I watched the vehicle approaching from the east and thought this might be a good opportunity for me to make an example of

G.L. Holmes

some oil field boys. As the pickup came into focus, through the cloud of caliche dust, I felt a wave of electricity surge out to the end of my tail and bounce back.

Holy smokes, that wasn't oil field traffic, it was the pickup that belonged to *Beulah's ranch*!

And she was riding in the back!

CHAPTER
6

AN UNEXPECTED TRIP INTO SPOOK CANYON

Mercy! All at once I felt as giddy as a pup. I mean, consider the opportunity that was about to fall into my lap. Here was the woman of my dreams, my one and only true love, the world's most beautiful collie dog, coming down *my* road in a pickup that I could bark all the way to the next cattle guard.

If I had been the least bit inclined to show off in front of women, this provided me with the perfect opportunity. And while I wasn't one to cast my pearls before oysters, so to speak, or to engage in childish displays for the benefit of just any old girl-dog, Beulah wasn't just any old girl-dog.

No way could I pass up this chance to show her my best stuff.

See, there were sides of my personality she had never seen. Basically and fundamentally, down at the bottom of the soil of experience where the roots of my complex personality lay pulling in the nutrients of . . .

Lost my train of thought there.

Something about plants.

Huh. Just lost it.

Anyway, I guess I was talking about plants. In the past sixty days I had noticed an increase in vegetation in the ditches along my road—Johnson grass, thistles, wild flowers, and . . .

Oh yeah, Beulah. She was coming down the road in Billy's pickup. Hot dog, what an opportunity! I stood in the middle of the road and waited.

You ever notice that on a hot day, pickups turn soupy? I know that sounds strange, but I've observed it many times. At a distance, maybe half a mile away, the front end of a pickup will turn to soup or water or something wavy and fuzzy. When it gets up close, it goes back to steel, but at a distance it looks just like chicken broth. It won't do that in cold weather, but on a hot day it happens all the time.

I've often wondered if ordinary dogs notice such small details. It must be some special power I have. Just thought I'd throw that in because when I first saw Beulah's pickup, it was soupy.

Billy was taking his time, driving slow, which fit right into my plan. He came toward me, closing the gap between us. Fifty feet out, he blew his horn—a hint, I suppose, for me to get out of the middle of the road. *My* road.

Heh. He didn't understand my strategy. You never saw a bullfighter step out of the path of bull, did you? No sir. The trick, if you can do it, is to wait until the last possible second, make your audience think there's no escape, throw a good scare into 'em, and then put a couple of fancy moves together and escape death by the thickness of a hair.

That's just what I did. Very slick move. No ordinary dog could have pulled that one off. It helped a little that Billy swerved into the ditch and derned near clipped the mail box, but I would have side-stepped him even if he hadn't.

Very slick move, though Billy didn't appreciate it . . . He bellered like a wounded rhinoceros and called me things my ma never taught me.

Beulah was standing on the spare tire, saw the whole thing. Boy, was she impressed! Plato was there too. Same story, very impressed. I fell in behind the pickup and chased after it.

"What did you think of that?"

Beulah wasn't smiling. "It looked very foolish to me. You could have gotten us killed!"

Plato spoke up. "That's a good point, Hank, and I'm sure you'll agree that one of the risks of exhibitionism . . ."

"Why don't you dry up!"

"Right. But I thought I should point out . . ."

"Hey Beulah, watch this." I did a few dives in the air, barking at the same time. "You ever run into another dog who could do that little trick?"

They looked at each other and shook their heads. Of course they hadn't! Nobody had. This was all new material.

"But this next one's going to knock your socks off," I yelled. "Just sit back and enjoy the show."

I turned on a sudden burst of speed and zoomed around to the side of the pickup. Old Billy was glaring down at me, talking under his breath. "Come on up here, soup hound, just a little closer."

As a matter of fact, that was exactly what I had on my agenda. I turned on some heavy barking, sprinted forward, and made a slash at his front tire. He blew his horn and swerved to the left. Did he think he could catch me unawares and roll me? Ha!

Behind me, I could hear Beulah's voice. "Hank, be careful, don't get yourself hurt showing off!"

"She's right, Hank, that looks risky to me." That was Mr. Echo, the bird dog.

The sound of Beulah's voice just by George inspired me to do incredible things. I was ready to move mountains, fight wildcats, swim rivers, jump canyons, tear down trees, the whole nine yards of amazing things a guy can do for that one special woman in his life. And the dangerouser, the better.

Even old Billy was impressed, in spite of himself. I know because I heard him say, "Try that one more time, doggie, come on, go for that tire just one more time."

I was a little winded after burning up the road and doing all that serious barking, but hey, when they're begging for an encore, what can you do? I turned on one last burst of speed and zoomed in to take a snap at the left front . . .

HUH?

It was a very sneaky and devious thing that

he did, one of the sneakiest, deviousest, foulest tricks that had ever been sprung on me. I fell for it—literally *fell* for it.

Here's what the snevious deak did to me, the devious sneak. First, he *asked* me to bite his tire, right? Okay, so I did that, made a dive for the tire. Suddenly he stomped the gas and sped up, which put me beside his door instead of beside the front tire.

Here's the clinker. *He opened his door, struck me in the rib cage, and sent me rolling into the ditch,* which just happened to be very deep since it connected to one of the draws leading into Spook Canyon. What's more, I think he did it on purpose.

Well fellers, it was flying lessons for this dog. There must have been five bottoms to that draw and I hit every stinking one of them and kept rolling. Oh rocks and brambles! Oh hurt!

When I returned to my senses, I was lying at the bottom of the ravine, not far from the creek and only a couple of steps east of Death's Door, so to speak.

I opened my eyes and looked into the tragic face of a bassett hound whose ears hung down to the level of his jowls which hung down to the level of his front paws which were pointed outward. That's a strange way to build a dog.

"Tender juicy chicken," I said.

"Potatoes and gravy," he said in his slow-talking voice.

I studied his face. "What do you mean by that?"

"Oh, just trying to make conversation. Was it you that come flying off that hill?"

I looked up at the hill, which loomed some seventy-five feet above us. "Yes, I'm the one."

"Thought maybe you was. Heard all the racket and come over here to check. Thought maybe you took a tumble, the way it looked. Are you hurt?"

"What do you think?"

"Well . . ." He was a slow thinker. Several minutes passed before he finished the sentence. ". . . I 'spect so."

I pushed myself up to a sitting position. "Everything hurts. A lesser dog wouldn't have survived that fall." I took another sweep of his face. There was something familiar about it. "Do I know you?"

"Yup. We served time together at the T.D.P."

"Texas Department of . . . what?"

"Twitchell Dog Pound. You was there on suspicion of hydrophobia."

"Oh yes, it's coming back now."

He sniffed his nose. "You had eat a bar of soap. Made your mouth foam."

"Yes indeed. That was the day I broke out and ran for my life. Let's see, they were going

G.L. Holmes

to cut off my head and send it to the state lab in Houston."

"Austin."

"And to make my escape, I had to flatten a cyclone fence."

"Well, you sure tried."

"Yes, I tried and succeeded. I can still hear the sound of snapping metal."

"A guy's memory plays tricks on him."

"Exactly. I can hear it, just as though it happened yesterday."

"That snapping sound was your neck when you hit the fence."

"Yes, it's all coming back now. What an adventure that was!"

"Uh huh."

"And let's see, your name is Clyde, as I recall, yes I'm sure it is because I remember thinking that you looked like a Clyde."

"Ralph."

"No, it was Clyde."

"Ralph."

"Hey listen, I'm the one who's remembering this story."

"Yeah, but I'm the one who knows what my name is."

Neither of us blinked for a long time. It was a tense moment. "All right, if you want to call yourself Ralph, that's no skin off my nose. But you and I both know that your real name is Clyde. The question is, why did you suddenly decide to change it?''

He wagged his head, causing his ears to flop. "I been Ralph since I was a pup. Never been Clyde in my whole life.''

I managed a laugh. "Come on, Ralph, the party's over. It took me a minute to put everything together but I've got it now. *You're under arrest for murder*!''

7

A BRILLIANT INTERROGATION OF A DIFFICULT SUSPECT

As you might have suspected, that caught him completely by surprise, which was no accident. I use stealth and cunning whenever possible, brute force only as a last resort.

He licked his chops and looked at me with those big sad eyes, which were even bigger and sadder now that I had confronted him with his bloody deeds.

"How come I'm under arrest?"

I stood up and worked a kink out of my back. Then I began pacing. I think better on my feet, don't you see, but on this occasion thinking on my feet turned out to be no ball of wax. I had taken a nasty fall, and the simple act of pacing required effort.

"My suspicions were aroused by the first words you said to me, something about 'tender juicy chicken'."

"I think *you* said that."

"Don't interrupt. The next clue emerged when I realized where we'd met. You're a con, Clyde, a jailhouse dog with a record as long as a piece of string."

"Yeah, but . . ."

"We've had two murders on the ranch, you see. Then a con with a crinimal record suddenly shows up. Interesting coincidence, wouldn't you say?"

"Never thought about it."

"The next tip-off came when, through clever interrogation, I learned that you had changed your name and were operating under a false identity."

"I already told you . . ."

"It was a smart trick, Clyde, and it took me a couple of minutes to pick it up. It would have worked on most dogs, but it was your bad luck to go up against one of the best in the business."

Clyde swept his eyes to the left and right.

"Where is he?"

"That's very funny, Clyde, but I'm afraid it won't get you out of this one. You're in this thing up to your ears and . . . do you ever step on those ears when you walk?"

"Oh, every now and then. Sure makes a guy feel awkward."

"Umm, yes. Tell me, Clyde," I closed my eyes and paced away from him, "do these feelings of insecuriority bother you a lot, a little, or you may have a third choice?"

"Only when I step on my ears. Makes me feel awkward."

"I understand. Now listen carefully and give me complete answers. When you're in the grip of these moods, do you find yourself dreaming of, shall we say, outrageous things or wreckless deeds?"

"Nope."

"Of course you do."

"Oh. Well, let me think." He eased himself down into the grass, crossed his paws in front of him, and rested his chin on them. I observed every movement, every gesture out of the corner of my eye. "Sometimes I wish I was a bird."

"What kind of bird?"

"A duck."

"Hmmm. Why do you wish you were a duck?"

"Well, a duck can fly in the air and swim in the water and walk on dry land. And they don't have big ears. Always thought that sounded like a pretty good deal."

"I see. We're getting very close, Clyde, and I must have your complete cooperation on this next question. How does your dream of being a duck relate to acts of violence and bloodshed?"

"Well, I don't know. Let me think about it."

"Think about it, Clyde, take your time. I want to do this case right."

He closed one eye, and I noticed that the other one rolled back in his head. Seemed strange to me. Most dogs think with their eyes open, but we all have our peculiar ways. I waited. And waited. And waited. He was asleep.

"Time's up, Clyde. What's your answer?"

He opened his eyes. "Fish emulsion."

"And how does fishy mullshun relate to your dream of becoming a duck?"

His eyes came into focus. "What are you talking about?"

"Murder."

He blinked. "I must have missed something."

"Yes, and let the record so state. You were talking, Clyde . . ."

"Ralph."

". . . . about your fantasy of becoming a violent, blood-thirsty duck because your ears are too long."

"That sounds crazy."

I smiled and arched one brow. "You said it, Clyde, I didn't. Don't accuse me of putting words in your mouth."

"Okay."

"Tell me more about your homicidal fantasies. What else do you dream about?"

"Well, I dream about food."

"Ah ha! Go on, tell me more. What kinds of food?"

"Oh, let's see. Dog kernels, dog biscuits, dog burgers, chunky dog food in a can with gravy, steak bones, pork chop bones, chicken bones . . ."

"Stop!"

"Huh?"

I walked over to him. "Isn't it amazing, Clyde, how the crinimal mind works? Were you aware, for example, that you put chicken bones at the *end* of your list?"

"Well, I really wasn't finished."

"Of course you were. And you put chicken bones at the very end, where you assumed I wouldn't notice. But of course you couldn't have known that I always ignore beginnings and middles and wait like a coyote on a rabbit trail for the last item on the list to come hopping by. How could you have known that?"

"Search me."

"Exactly what I've been doing, Clyde, searching you, searching your mind, your dreams, your fantasies, your attempts to shield yourself from the dreadful truth."

"What is the dreadful truth?"

"Not yet, be patient." I paced away. "In this next procedure, I'm going to throw a series of words at you. I want you to answer immediately with the first thought that pops into your head. Ready? Here we go. Dream."

"Cream."

"Duck."

"Pluck."

"Bone."

"Stone."

I paced over and looked down into his mournful face. "I don't think you understand, Clyde. This isn't a rhyming exercise. It's a serious procedure that brings the awful truth to the surface. Don't give me rhymes, in other words."

"Oh, okay."

"Ready? Here we go."

To avoid confusion, I'll record this next segment of the interrogation in transcript form.

Hank: "Feathers."

Clyde: "Uh . . . bird."

Hank: "Blood."

Clyde: "Guts."

Hank: "Murder."

Clyde: "Mystery."

Hank: "Chicken."

Clyde: "Squawk."

Hank: "Juicy."

Clyde: "Steak."

Hank: "Tender."

Clyde: "Carbuncle."

Hank: "Drool."

Clyde: "Slobber."

Hank: "I love it!"

Clyde: "Dog biscuits."

Hank: "Can't wait!"

Clyde: "Uh . . ."

Hank: "Young, tender, juicy chicken, lar-ruping good, holy smokes!"

Clyde: "Uh . . . give me some time on that one . . ."

Hank: "Stop! No more, I can't stand it!"

I staggered several steps away and slumped against a tree. Suddenly I felt light-headed and faint. My pulse was racing and I could feel my eyes bulging on every heart beat. And I was drooling at the mouth.

Clyde was watching me. His jowls drooped, his ears drooped, his entire face drooped. "What's the trouble?"

I took a deep, trembling breath and closed my eyes. "I . . . I'm not sure. All of a sudden everything just . . . I'm not well, Clyde."

"Ralph."

My eyes popped open. "You really are Ralph, aren't you?"

"Uh huh."

"What are you doing down here?"

"Came fishing with Jimmy Joe the Dog Catcher."

"I was afraid of that. Do you know what this means?"

"Fish don't bite after a rain."

"No. It means my entire case has collapsed. Hours and days of work, all for nothing."

"Gosh, I'm sure sorry."

"You're not entirely to blame. But then," I stood up, took a deep breath, and smiled a brave smile, "but then I can't very well blame myself, can I?"

"Reckon not."

"And so the mystery slips behind the veil

once more. Well! You're free to go, Ralph. I have no evidence, no case. I can't hold you any longer.''

"Guess I'll go see if Jimmy Joe's caught any fish.''

"Yes, do that, Ralph. Have fun for both of us. It must be nice to enjoy simple things.''

"It's perty good. See you around, Hank, and I hope you catch the killer.''

"Ummm, indeed . . . yes.''

C H A P T E R

8

ON TRIAL IN THE HORSE PASTURE

Ralph left and I made my way back toward headquarters. I hobbled down the creek a ways until I came to the place where the horses had worn a path up the hill, then I dragged myself up on top.

I had come down that hill a lot faster than I went up it, which explained why I was hobbling and dragging around. Sure was sore.

I got to the top of the hill and stopped to catch my breath and rest my bones and let the wind blow my ears around. Down below, I could see Ralph making his way up the creek toward a man who was fishing on the bank.

Ralph and his big ears had certainly ruined my case. Just when I'd thought the clues were lined up and moving in the right direction, he'd started yapping about fresh, young, tender, juicy, larruping good chick . . . never mind, just never mind. There was something about those words that . . . never mind again.

I started back to headquarters, keeping to the ditch beside the county road. A big tank truck came along, blowing dark smoke out the two chimneys above the cab. Under ordinary conditions, I would have barked him off the ranch, but I was too sore to get myself worked up into a good mad. I just sat in the ditch and glared at him as he roared past.

I went on down the road, limping and counting my miseries, when I heard hoof beats in the distance. I looked around and saw the entire horse herd coming my way, the work string as well as the brood mares. I hoped they were going to water and hadn't seen me, and I crouched down in the grass.

I have no use for horses, just don't like 'em. They've got this superior attitude, see, that makes them hard to take even on a good day. And so far, this hadn't been one of my better days.

They came kicking and bucking down the hill. I stretched out flat on the ground and directed all my powers of concentration toward making myself invisible. Horses don't have such good eyes, don't you know, and they can be fooled.

The next thing I knew, I was surrounded by thirteen head of horses, which just goes to show that sometimes they *can't* be fooled. I didn't move, just rolled my eyes around the circle of horse heads. You don't realize how big they are until you've got thirteen of them standing over you.

I figgered maybe they had seen me and there was no use trying to hide any more. "Afternoon," I said.

Silence. Then a cocky, stocky bay horse named Casey spoke up. "Say, puppy, you know where you are?"

I looked around. "Uh, let's see. There's the barn over there . . ."

"You in the horse pasture, son. You in our place. You in trouble."

"That so?" I pushed myself up to a sitting position. "Well, maybe you don't remember who I am."

"You're the ranch mutt, ain't you?"

"No, you're thinking of Drover—short-haired, stub-tailed little white dog."

"No, I'm thinking of you, puppy."

"In that case you must know that I'm Hank the Cowdog, Head of Ranch Security." For some reason, they all laughed. "Did I say something funny?"

Casey wore a sneer on his big flappy mouth. "Son, you may be a hot dog over on your side of the fence, but you in the horse pasture now, and in the horse pasture, hey, if you ain't a horse, you ain't nuthin'."

"That's just your opinion, of course. In my circles we think just the opposite."

Casey bent his head down. "Explain what you mean by that."

"Well uh, we often say that if you ain't nuthin', you can't possibly be a horse. I'm sure you'd go along with that."

He gave me a blank stare. Then he grinned and exposed two rows of the biggest teeth I'd ever seen. "But the point is, you in the wrong place and we don't like dogs."

"I can understand that. I've met a few I didn't like either. There's good and bad in every breed. I'm sure you'd go along with that." He shook his head. "Or maybe you wouldn't."

I was beginning to feel a little lonesome there in the middle of all those horses and figgered it was time to check out the escape routes. It appeared to me that every exit passed between a horse's legs, which wasn't too encouraging.

A guy could get his back stepped on trying to escape, which is probably why the old-timers used to say, "Don't put all your backs in one exit." Might get stepped on, see.

"You know what we do with dogs that get into our pasture?" asked Casey.

"No, I don't, but maybe I should point something out here . . ."

"We bite 'em. We push 'em around with our noses. We step on their tails."

"Maybe you've forgotten that I have clearance to work this entire ranch, including the horse pasture."

"Heh." Casey looked around the circle. "All right, y'all, we got us a dog here, accused of trespassing. This court is now in session."

"Now hold on just a . . ."

"Does the defendant have anything to say?"

I stood up. "Yes, as a matter of fact, I . . ."

"Sit down, son. The defense rests its case. No further questions. Now, let the prosecution present its case."

A big brown horse named Popeye stepped out. "He's guilty."

"You sure?"

"Yup."

Casey looked down at me and shook his head. "Puppy, looks like the evidence in this case is just overwhelming."

I looked around the circle of eyes. All the horses were stamping at flies and swishing their tails. I pinned my ears back and growled. "You can't get by with this." That was the best I could come up with.

Casey turned to his pals. "After hearing all the evidence in this case and giving this pup a fair trial, we find him guilty of trespassing in the horse pasture. What shall the sentence be?"

"Bite him."

"Bite him."

"Bite him!"

By this time the hair was standing up on my back and deep growls were rumbling up from my throat. "I'd advise you guys to keep your distance, because the first horse that . . ."

At that very moment one of the horses behind me bent down and bit me on the bohunkus. I jumped straight up and squalled, wheeled around and bit him right back on the nose. Another one got me on the back. I nailed him, but by that time they were coming from all directions.

I was by George surrounded, and while I'm

fairly comfortable with odds of five- or six-to-one, this fight showed signs of getting out of hand. It was time to light a shuck and get the heck out of there.

I tore into them, knocked three or four of 'em to the ground, and literally clawed and gnawed my way to daylight. With three head of horses on my tail, I sprinted across open ground toward the home pasture and ducked under the barbed wire fence just in the nick of time.

G. L. Holmes

With the fence between us, I turned to Casey and Popeye and Happy. "Let that be a lesson to you!" They laughed. "Next time, you won't get off so easy." They laughed harder.

There's no future in trying to talk to a bunch of danged smart alecky horses. I had made my point and throwed a good scare into 'em and I didn't have time for any more foolishness. I had work to do.

It took me a good five minutes to lick down all the spots where they'd bit me and made my hair stand up, and there was one place in the middle of my back that I couldn't quite reach. I bent my neck as far around as it would go, extended my tongue to its maximum length, and walked around in circles trying to get a good lick at it. But every time I moved, *it* moved, and it managed to stay just a few inches beyond the reach of my tongue.

This was very frustrating. I try to keep my coat neat, don't you know, and I don't like to go around looking like the rats had chewed on me all night. I chased that derned spot until my tongue got tired and my head was spinning. Never did get it, had to roll in some mud to smooth it down.

I hopped up and gave myself a good shake, scratched a spot just below my left ear and tried to recall what I'd been working on before that maniac cowboy had hit me with his pickup door and knocked me into Spook Canyon.

Let's see: Ralph . . . the mailman . . . the horses . . . Beulah, mercy me, I could still see her gorgeous collie ears flapping in the wind as I ran along beside the pickup, and her perfect collie nose, and her brown eyes melting in adoration as she watched her hero perform death-defying tricks that no ordinary dog, especially Plato, could have matched.

Why, at that very moment she was probably gazing into the distance and sobbing, wondering if the love of her life had survived his plunge off the cliff. No doubt she had tried to leap out of the pickup and rush to my side, but Plato had stopped her. I could almost hear it:

"No Beulah, I can't let you do this."

"Let me go, he needs me!"

"But you could be killed, jumping out of a moving pickup."

"Better to die in love than to live in anguish. I leap now into the great unknown, to join my beloved cowdog who lieth wounded and bleeding and calleth my name!"

"Don't be foolish, Beulah!"

"Unhand me, I must go to him!"

"No, I can't allow it!"

Etc.

Actually, Plato was right in stopping her. She might have broken a leg jumping out of the pickup. It's amazing, what a woman in love will do. And just think: she was ready to do all that *just for me!* Kind of makes a guy wonder what it is about himself that gets the ladies so stirred up. Good looks are part of the answer, but there's bound to be more to it than that.

Well, I was in the midst of these delicious thoughts when it suddenly occurred to me that when I'd left my post several hours ago, I had been involved in a very serious investigation, The Case of the Vanishing Chickens. Ordinarily, I'm not easily distracted, and yet . . . I had been distracted easily.

Well, I had wasted enough time with women and jail house dogs and horses and the mailman. I had work to do, clues to find, suspects to interrogate—and a murderer to catch.

C H A P T E R

9

DROVER CONFESSES

I set my sights on headquarters and turned on the speed. I roared past those big rolls of rusted barbed wire and the post pile. I was kind of sore at myself for burning so much daylight and . . . was that a cottontail rabbit that came out of the post pile?

I put on the brakes and slid to a stop. Indeed it was, a nice plump little cottontail, and I've seen very few days when I was so prosperous that I wouldn't give a cottontail a run. I wheeled around and went after him.

As I closed the gap on him, he just stood there like a little statue, the way a cottontail will do when he thinks he's invisible in the grass. That was just fine. I took two final jumps, leaped through the air, and landed right in the middle of him.

I lifted one paw and he wasn't there. I lifted the other paw and he wasn't there again. Hmm. I glanced around and saw him about five feet to the north, sitting as stiff as a post with his ears pointed up.

Okay, he wanted to be clever, I could be clever too. I stood up and shook my head—that was to throw him off, see, make him think I was confused. Then I sat down and scratched my ear, but as you may have already guessed, I watched him out of the corner of my eye. It was all part of my clever plan.

But you know what? Once I got to scratching on that ear, it felt so good I didn't want to quit. I found a spot there that probably hadn't been scratched in years, and I just can't describe how good it felt.

First I scratched it real hard. Then I kind of leaned my head into my paw and rubbed it from both ends. It sent delicious tingling sensations down my back and out to the end of my tail, felt so derned good that my eyes started drooping.

It's funny. All his life a guy looks for happiness and contentment. He looks for it in his work and his love life, and he tends to overlook the little things, like scratching a certain spot just above his ear.

Well, I scratched and I rubbed, and I rubbed and I scratched, and my eyelids drooped and I relaxed all over, and after a while I just kind of melted—fell over backwards, you might say. I lay there for a long time, looking up at the puffy white clouds and blinking my eyes.

Then I jumped up and shook the grass off my coat and . . . HUH? My head snapped around, just in time to see that sniveling little cottontail hop into one of the pipes in the cattleguard. In other words, I had wasted more time and burned more daylight, fooling around with a dadgum rabbit.

G.L.Holmes

I headed for the machine shed. In this business, you've got to be alert all the time. You've got to concentrate on your objective and shut the little distractions out of your mind, because no matter how you look at it, the little things in this life are still little, and it takes a special kind of dog . . . never mind.

Before I reached headquarters, I had already reviewed the case in my mind. Last night: one murder. This morning: a second murder. Suspects: zero. Clues: none. Overall status of case in progress: not so good.

I won't say that my whole career was riding on this case, because after all, I had enjoyed a rather glorious career and had solved many mysteries. But if I didn't break this case pretty quick, it wouldn't look good.

I slowed down and coasted up to the machine shed. High Loper and Drover were standing in the door, and I went over to them. When Loper saw me coming, he narrowed his eyes and said, "Here he comes now."

I didn't like the sound of that.

He told us to sit down and he went into the machine shed. While he was gone, I turned to Drover. "What's up?"

He looked up and squinted at the sky. "Well . . ."

"What's Loper got on his mind?"

"Oh. Oh-h-h Hank, he found the feathers down by the creek and he knows about the chicken murders!"

That was a piece of bad news. I had hoped to have the case wrapped up before he found out about it.

Just then, Loper came out of the machine shed. He had a brown paper bag in his hand and a very unfriendly expression on his face. He glared down at us and rocked up and down on his toes. Drover was so nervous, he tried to hide behind Loper's leg.

Loper opened up the bag and pulled out a handful of feathers. He held them out for us to smell. I smelled. Drover ducked his head, squirmed around in a circle, and wagged his stub tail. Drover gets very uncomfortable when he can't run to the machine shed and hide from life's tribulations.

"Somebody's been killing chickens around here," said Loper. "I don't know who did it. Maybe it was coons. Maybe it was a skunk. Maybe it was coyotes. I don't know, but I want you dogs to put a stop to it, you hear?"

I whapped my tail against the ground. Drover rolled on his back and held his paws up in the beg position.

"Of course," Loper shifted his chewing tobacco over to the other cheek, "there's one other possibility." He looked at me and I

G.L. Holmes

whapped my tail. "Sometimes *dogs* turn to chicken-killing."

Well, that was news to me. I'd never heard of such a thing.

"And do you know what happens to chicken-killing dogs?" I looked away and whapped my tail. "They have to be shot. There's no other cure. Once a dog gets the taste of chicken, it makes him a little crazy."

It suddenly occurred to me that *Drover* was acting "a little crazy." I mean, he was oozing guilt. Was it possible . . . could it be that . . . I couldn't bring myself to put the pieces of the puzzle together and follow the logic to this conclusion. It was just too awful. And yet . . .

Why was he rolling around that way? Why did he have that silly grin on his face? And come to think of it, where had he been when the murders had been discovered?

As I studied the little mutt, my heart sank. I've said before that to be in the security business, you have to be made from a special kind of steel, but nothing I'd ever done in my career had prepared me for this.

Loper stuffed the feathers back into the sack, shook it in my face and then shook it in Drover's. "No more chicken killing on this ranch or somebody's head is going to roll, you got that?'' He stormed back into the machine shed and left us alone.

We got away from there, went down to the gas tanks. Drover was still trembling all over. ''Boy, that was scary! I sure hope we don't lose any more chickens.''

I studied him out of the corner of my eye. He was still behaving in a strange manner. ''How come you got so nervous up there, Drover?''

''Well, gosh, Loper was mad and . . .''

''Yes, but if you didn't do anything wrong, why should you get so antsy about it? You weren't by any chance feeling guilty, were you?''

''Well . . . maybe I was.''

''I see.'' I began pacing. ''And why were you feeling guilty, Drover? Just tell me in your own words.''

''My own words. Okay. Let's see. Guilty. I don't know.''

''Are those your own words?''

''I think so.''

''Then think a little deeper. Why were you feeling guilty about something you didn't do?''

He rolled his eyes and twisted his head to one side. ''Well, I always feel guilty, Hank. Every morning when I wake up, the first thing I do is feel guilty."

"There must be a reason for it."

"Well . . . I mess up a lot. Do you suppose that could be it?"

"I'll ask the questions. You give the answers."

"Oh. All right."

I waited and waited. Nothing. "Well?"

"Sure turned out to be a pretty day, didn't it?"

I paced over in front of him. "You're being slippery, Drover, but I'm afraid that won't wash. I'll ask you again. Why do you feel guilty every morning when you wake up?"

"Well . . . I think of all the things I can mess up during the day and . . ."

"Yes? Go on."

". . . and it makes me feel awful. Then when I mess up for real, I don't have to worry about it." He looked at me with a simple grin on his mouth, as though he had just said something wonderful.

I stopped pacing and went nose-to-nose with the runt. "That makes no sense at all, and furthermore, it has nothing to do with the Case of the Vanishing Chickens."

"Oh."

"I want to know why you were acting so guilty when Loper was talking about the murders."

"Well . . ."

I sensed that I was very close to a confession. It was time to bore in with my toughest questions and break down his resistance. I had a suspicion that three or four questions would wrap the case up.

"Is it possible, Drover, that there's a side to your personality we don't know about? That on very short notice, you can change from being a simple buffoon into a chicken killer? That you have a secret craving for chicken meat? And finally . . . what are you staring at?"

"You've got four little circles of hair sticking up on your back."

"What?" I bent my neck around and looked at my back. Sure enough, I saw four little circles of hair sticking up. "Oh. That's where the horses bit me. I was attacked by the entire horse herd a while ago."

"Oh my gosh!"

"I was working traffic, barked a pickup into the horse pasture, and the horses jumped me. If you'd been up there helping me, it never would have happened."

"Oh gosh."

"But you were hiding in the machine shed . . ."

His head began to sink. "Yes."

". . . after you saw Sally May coming down to the garden."

He began to cry. "It's true."

"You ran to save your own skin and left me alone."

"Yes!"

"And you cowered in the machine shed while I was being mauled by thirteen dog-eating horses!"

"Yes, I did, Hank!"

I looked down at him. My questions had reduced him to jelly. "So you admit your guilt?"

"Yes!" He was bawling now, and the tears were dripping off the end of his nose. "It was all my fault, and I feel so guilty I can hardly stand it!"

Sometimes I'm frightened by my own inter-rogations. I mean, when a guy can break a sus-pect down with just a few devastating ques-tions, reduce him to tears in a matter of minutes—that's awesome. There's no other word for it.

I couldn't help feeling sorry for Drover. I

hadn't wanted to give him the full load of devastating questions, but I'd had no choice. I didn't want to watch him cry, so I walked off a little ways and waited for him to pull himself back together.

I mean, I had won. I could afford to be decent about it. I had gotten a confession out of him and had pretty muchly wrapped up . . .

HUH? Wait a minute.

I whirled around. "Hey Drover . . ."

He had disappeared.

I had a confession, all right, but a confession of *what*?

10

A NEW TWIST IN
THE CASE

I went looking for Drover and checked all his usual hiding spots: the machine shed, the calf shed, the hay stack. He wasn't there. The runt had given me the slip—and maybe he'd done it in more ways than one.

As I've said before, Drover is a special case. Just when you're convinced that his head is filled with sawdust, he comes up with some slippery move that has the markings of intelligent behavior. It certainly makes a guy wonder.

But slippery moves or not, he remained a prime suspect in the investigation. When you're going up against Hank the Cowdog, you can run but you can't walk. It takes more than a few tricks to throw me off the trail. I made a mental note to keep my assistant under surveillance.

I drifted through the corrals, figgered while I was down there I might as well make my rounds and check things out.

I went past the calf shed and slipped through the warped door of the hay barn. As usual, it was dark and smelled of alfalfa hay and . . . hmmm. Near the northwest corner I began picking up a new reading. In just a matter of minutes I had analyzed the smell, separated out the many variables and possibilities, and narrowed it down to one source: skunk.

Very interesting. In fact, VERY interesting. Point One: It's a well known fact that skunks have an appetite for eggs and chickens. Point Two: They're smell enough . . . small enough to enter a chicken house through the little door. Point Three: They have sharp teeth and are quite capable of killing a chicken. Point Four: Having killed the chicken inside the chicken house, they are stout enough to drag the body outside. Point Five: I don't think there is a Point Five, but four's plenty.

This discovery had just by George blown the case wide open. I couldn't have ordered a set of clues that would have worked better than these. Everything fit the M.O. All at once I had a scent, a motive, and a suspect.

Well, I didn't exactly have a suspect. A quick check of the premises revealed that he was no longer there, but in his scent I had irreguffable proof that he HAD been there, and not so very long ago—say, last night, just after he committed the first murder, and this morning, just before he committed the second.

G. L. Holmes

Yes indeed, things were moving along very well. I slithered out the door and gave my eyes a minute to adjust to the glare of the afternoon sun. A plan began to form in my mind. I had one last witness to interrogate, and then all I had to do was wait for darkness to fall. If the killer struck again, I would be waiting for him.

I trotted through the front lot, through the side lot, through the wire lot. I passed the old green outhouse, ran up the hill, and made my way to the chicken house. I found my witness in some weeds near the storage tank, chasing grasshoppers. J.T. Cluck, head rooster, just might have some information I could use.

I came up behind him and waited for him to see me. He was so absorbed in his grasshopper business that he didn't notice me. Finally I got tired of hanging around. I mean, I have better things to do than wait for a dadgum rooster.

"Hey!"

His head shot up. He squawked, flapped his wings, and jumped off the ground a good ten inches. "Bawk! Help, murder! Oh, it's only you."

"That's right, it's only me, if that's the way you want to put it. I've got some questions to ask you."

"All right, fine, because I've got some questions to ask you too."

"Who goes first?"

"I'll go first."

"All right, and I'll go second. Shoot, and don't waste my time with gossip or insignificant details. And I don't want to hear about your worthless sons."

He jerked his head and fixed me with one of his yellow eyes. "Who said my sons were worthless? Just point him out to me and I'll thrash the lying scoundrel!"

"You've said it. Every time I'm around you, that's all you can talk about."

"It's all right for me to say that, but anybody else who says it is going to get thrashed. I have some fine boys."

"Good."

"Elsa has done a wonderful job raising them."

"I'm so happy for you."

"And if they do act a little worthless now and then, it ain't her fault."

"Of course not."

"Because she done her part."

"What's your question?"

"What? Oh, my question, yes." He glanced

over both shoulders and moved closer. "How much do you know about grasshoppers?"

"Not much."

"Well, let me tell you something. I don't ever recall seeing a crop of grasshoppers that could jump as far as these, and I've been studying grasshoppers for many years. If you ask me, there's something strange going on around here. I think maybe this climate's changing,

G.L. Holmes

makes the grasshoppers harder to catch. It won't be long until we all starve to death."

"Maybe you're getting too old. Had you considered that?"

"Huh? Too old? Who said that! Let me tell you something, mister. I may be getting a little age on me, but that's only because I ain't as young as I used to be, and don't you ever forget it."

"Okay. Are you through?"

"Naw, I'm just getting warmed up."

"No, I think you're through. It's my turn."

He glared at me. "Kind of grabby, ain't you?"

"Just doing my job. Now, I've got some questions."

"Fine. Ask me anything, anything at all. Ask me about grasshoppers or indigestion, I've had terrible heartburn lately."

"I don't care about indigestion."

"That's the whole trouble with this younger generation, they just don't care about anything."

"I presume you're aware that two of your pullets have been murdered."

"Of course I'm aware of it. What kind of fiend do you think I am?"

"I'm working on the case and I need some facts. You got any facts for me?"

"Yes sir, I sure do." He tapped me on the chest with his wing. "Fact Number One: If you don't get enough gravel in your craw, you're going to get heartburn. Elsa's been telling me that for years, but I get so busy with other stuff that I can't remember to peck gravel, just can't be bothered with it."

"Never mind the gravel. I want facts about the murders."

"What murders? Oh, those. You know what I think?"

"No. Why don't you tell me?"

"I think we've got a fiendish, blood-thirsty, killing murderer on the loose, is what I think. Who else would kill a couple of pullets?"

"I've got a lead on a skunk. You smelled any skunks lately?"

He narrowed his eyes. "Who can smell a skunk in a filthy chicken house? I have to live in filth because these danged kids . . ."

"Have you *seen* any skunks? Have you seen anything . . ." All at once I noticed the shape of J.T.'s drumsticks. "Let me ask you something, J.T."

"Go on, ask me anything. My life's an open book, I got nothing to be ashamed of."

"When a chicken gets older, does the meat lose its flavor?"

"Oh yes, very definitely, and that's why nobody ever eats old roosters, see. Yes, we get a little age on us and that meat turns tough and stringy. You'd just as well try to eat a roll of binder's twine."

"I see."

"Very tough, very stringy, not much flavor. Now with an old hen, you can take and boil an old hen with some dumplings and she'll turn out all right. But an old rooster, no sir."

"I see." I ran my tongue over my lips. "And . . . pullets? What about pullets?"

"Oh, they're just about the best eatin' around. Now you take this meat up here around the chest. On a pullet that meat's nice and tender and juicy and . . ."

"And larruping good?"

"Yes sir, larruping good, that's what they tell me."

"And uh, how about the uh . . . drumsticks on a pullet?"

"Just excruciatingly good. Tender as a woman's heart, juicy as apple pie . . ." He blinked his eyes and stared at me. "What's wrong with your mouth, son?"

"Huh?"

"You got water coming out of your mouth. You're drooling all over yourself."

I turned away and wiped my mouth. "No, that's not drool. It's uh . . ."

"Sure looked like drool to me. Turn back around here and let me look at that again."

"I'm telling you, it's not drool. It has nothing to do with drool."

He dropped his voice. "You can't fool me, son."

Very slowly I turned my head around, until our eyes met. "What do you mean by that?"

"I mean, you can't fool the head rooster. You're drooling at the mouth, and I know what that means."

"Oh yeah? Well uh . . . what does it mean?"

I could hear my heart pounding in my . . . well, in my chest. For some reason, I dreaded his next words.

J.T. leaned toward me and whispered, *"You've been eatin' grasshoppers!"*

Just for a moment I felt dizzy. Then it passed and I took a deep breath. "How did you know that?"

"Simple deduction and years of experience. Grasshoppers spit tobacco juice, right? Which means they chew tobacco, right? Which means that when you eat a grasshopper, you're eating his tobacco juice, right? Well sir, that tobacco juice makes a guy drool at the mouth. I know because I've done it many, many times."

"It's very clever of you to figure that out."

"And I'll tell you something else." He put his beak right in my face. "That stuff will give you the most incredible heartburn you ever had in your life. Now take my advice and don't go slippin' around eatin' grasshoppers any more."

I wiped my mouth and regained my composure. "As a general rule I don't take advice from chickens, but in this case I'm going to make an exception."

"You could do a lot worse, believe me."

I started backing away. "Well, I think I've . . . uh . . . learned something from this interrogation, and if you'll excuse me, I have to get back to work."

"See you around, son," he waved a wing. "And don't forget your gravel—every morning and evening."

11

THE STING STINGS THE WRONG GUY

My interrogation of J.T. Cluck confirmed what I had already begun to suspect—in order to catch the murderer, I would have to do a stake-out of the chicken house.

In case you're not familiar with the technical language of the security business, to "stake out" a place simply means that we set up an observation point in a high crime area and wait for the villain to strike.

It's a very handy technique, but I should point out that we don't go to the stake-out until we've done a thorough investigation and have a suspect in mind.

At sundown, I found Drover down at the gas tanks and told him what I had in mind.

"Do you have a suspect?"

"I have several suspects, Drover, including some names you would recognize."

"Oh my gosh! I'm sure glad I'm not . . . Hank, I'm not on the list, am I?"

"At this point in the investigation, I'm not at liberty to say any more. Why?" I arched my brows and met his gaze. "Are you feeling guilty again?"

He began to fidget. "Well . . . yes, I am, but I don't know why I should. Do you ever feel guilty?"

I looked away and began to fidget. "Sometimes I . . . I'd better be going, Drover. In a couple of hours we should know something, one way or another."

"You don't want me to go with you?" I shook my head. "Oh my gosh, I hope I don't walk in my sleep."

"Yes, this would be a bad night for that. Well, so long, Drover." I started away, but he called me back.

"Hank, are *you* a suspect?"

I looked at him for a long time, then smiled. "Why do you ask a question like that?"

"Oh, it was just a crazy idea that popped into my head."

"The answer is yes, it *was* a crazy idea. So long."

After watching a brilliant sunset, I set up shop in some weeds exactly ten paces north of the chicken house. This gave me an unobstructed view of the door, so that no one could enter or leave without being seen.

By nine o'clock darkness had settled over the ranch. The chickens had gone to roost and their house was quiet except for an occasional coo or squawk. In the darkness and silence, I waited. And for some reason I felt uneasy.

I had never worked a case quite like this one, where one of the suspects included . . . well, Drover, for instance. Even though I had found evidence that cast suspicion on a certain skunk, I couldn't ignore Drover's guilty behavior. Nor, for that matter, could I entirely rule out . . .

One of the marks of your blue ribbon, top of the line cowdog is that he must know the truth, and he's willing to follow a line of evidence even when it leads into a dark pit of . . . knowing the truth is not always pleasant, don't you see, especially when it reveals . . . .

I had to find out who was behind the chicken house murders, even if it meant . . . I had to know, that's all. It was my job, but that didn't make it easy or pleasant.

The minutes dragged by. I listened to the

crickets and the frogs. I counted the stars. I waited and watched. At last I heard something: a small scratching sound. My eyes probed the darkness and my ears jumped to their full-alert position.

At first I thought I was dreaming, but then a skunk came waddling out of some weeds. He stopped, sniffed the air, looked around, listened, sniffed again, and waddled straight to the chicken house door.

My heart was pounding like a drum. I could hardly sit still. But I had to. I waited and watched.

What I saw and heard next is still hard for me to believe. The skunk lifted his head and began to sing a very strange and exotic tune that sent shivers up and down my backbone. I couldn't imagine why he was doing this, but then . . .

All at once, a pullet appeared at the chicken house door. Her eyes were closed and her head was drooped to the side, and she held her wings out in front of her. Holy cats, she was in a trance and the skunk had called her out with that strange tune!

The skunk kept singing. The pullet walked down the ramp, made an abrupt turn to the left, and began following the skunk in a westerly direction.

Well, I had seen enough. I had broken the case. Now I had to save the pullet before the skunk lured her into the weeds and gave her the bite of death.

I sprang out of my hiding place and went on the attack. The skunk heard me coming. He stopped singing and turned to face me. That was his first mistake. I drew back my right paw and slugged him square on the end of his nose, sent him flying through the weeds and rolling down the hill.

That took care of the skunk. Now I had to catch the chicken before she ran off into the night and got lost. The noise of my scuffle with the skunk had brought her out of her sleep, and in typical chicken behavior, she began squawking, flapping her wings, and running around in circles.

"Shhhhh! Be quiet, you idiot, you're going to wake up half the county!"

I don't know how long it took me to catch her—several minutes, I would guess, though it seemed like hours. Finally I caught her and started toward the chicken house. I had to be very careful in performing this maneuver, because . . . well, my big sharp teeth were directly in contact with her nice, tender, juicy . . . and it was hard to get a good grip because, for some odd reason, my mouth was . . . well, watering, you might say.

I had gotten so involved in chasing and catching the chicken that I hadn't heard the footsteps or seen the flashlight beam. Then suddenly there we were: Loper holding the flashlight and me holding the chicken.

"Oh no. Hank, how could you do this?"

HUH?

I set the chicken down, as if to say, "There we go, little gal, now you get yourself back to the house." Even so, I guess it looked pretty suspicious. I grinned up into the flashlight beam and whapped my tail.

"Come on, Hank." He started walking to the west, and I, being an obedient dog, followed. I thought maybe he was going to look for the skunk. No. He opened the door of the old green outhouse, grabbed me by the scruff of the neck, and throwed me inside.

He stood there, looking down at me for a long time. "You won't feel a thing, but it's going to tear me up something awful. I'm sorry, Hank. Tomorrow morning, me and you will take a little ride."

He slammed the door and I heard his foot-steps disappear into the night.

I couldn't believe it! I had seen it with my own eyes and heard it with my own ears, but I still couldn't believe it. Unless I had misunderstood, Loper thought *I was the chicken house murderer!* Why, that was just outrageous. How could he . . . I mean, his own Head of Ranch Security! If he had come just a few minutes sooner, he would have seen me fighting with the . . .

G. L. Holmes

All at once I realized that the most important piece of evidence in my defense was missing. *The skunk hadn't sprayed me.* I hadn't given him time. I had been too quick, too efficient in boxing him on the nose and saving the danged chicken, and now I had no witnesses and nothing to prove my innocence.

As I sat there in the spider-crawling darkness, it began to dawn on me that I had got myself in a mess of trouble. When Loper had said he would be taking me for a ride tomorrow morning, he had been talking about a one-way trip.

Hey, I had to get out of there, and fast! I studied my cell, searching for a weakness. There were no windows to leap out of. I threw myself against the door a couple of times and figgered out that Loper had locked it from the outside. And there wasn't much chance of me busting it down.

I sat down and was in the midst of feeling mighty sorry for myself when I heard something hit the roof with a thud. And then another thud. I stopped and listened. I heard voices. Somebody was up on the jail house roof!

No doubt some of my trusted friends had

gotten the news of my arrest and had come to bust me out of jail. But who might they be?

"Who's up there? Identify yourself."

There was a moment of silence, then "W-w-well, I'm J-J-Junior the B-Buzzard and . . ."

"You hush up, Junior, you're gonna fool around and mess up everything, you just snap your beak shut and let me do the talkin', if there's any talkin' to be done, which there ain't."

So . . . my "friends" turned out to be Wallace and Junior, the buzzards. When a guy gets down to buzzards, it means he's gone through his list of friends and has pretty muchly hit the bottom. As Wallace had once said, "A buzzard's only friend is his next meal."

But I had to try. "Say fellers, it's quite a coincidence, us running into each other in a place like this. Tell you what we might do, Junior. If you feel like singing a couple of songs, I might just crawl up on the roof with you guys . . ."

"Oh b-b-boy, I'd l-l-like that!"

"You hush your mouth, son!"

"But you might say that this door is locked, see, which makes it hard for me to go in and out. Now, if you fellers could just . . ."

"You can save your breath, dog, we ain't opening no doors. We come to have breakfast with you, and if there's any singing to be done, we'll handle it from up here, and you hush, Junior."

"Uh I d-d-didn't s-say anything, P-P-Pa."

"Well, hush up before you do, and then hush up again."

G.L. Holmes

"Thanks a lot, guys," I said. "I can't tell you how much I appreciate all your efforts and sacrifices." Silence. "Because I *don't* appreciate it. And one of these nights when you want to do some singing, you'll be sorry."

"He's r-r-right, P-Pa."

"Son, the world's full of singers. What we need is a good wholesome breakfast."

"B-b-but P-Pa, if you a-a-ask m-me . . ."

"I didn't, I haven't, I never will ask you. Now hush."

Well, that was that. I had given it my best shot and it hadn't gone anywhere. I curled up on the floor and tried to sleep, but sleep wouldn't come. What came instead of sleep was a song. I fought it as long as I could, then I sat up and sang it.

Locked In A Jail House

I'm locked in a jail house with buzzards on the
    roof.
In chasing the chicken, I think I really goofed.
It might have gone unnoticed if the chicken
    hadn't squawked,
Or if I'd bit her neck off, I doubt she would
    have talked.

123

These buzzards are omens that things have
gone astray.
They're waiting for their breakfast and they
won't go away.
From bird to bird I've tumbled from the
heights into this pen.
With chicken it got started, with buzzards it
will end.

I'm locked in the jail house with buzzards
standing by
Like black feathered tombstones, they wait for
me to die.
The sands of life are falling through the hour
glass of time
I cross my heart (and fingers), I didn't do this
crime!

In the silence I heard someone up on the
roof—sniffling, maybe even crying. Then
Junior said, "Oh, g-gosh, that was a p-p-pretty
s-s-s-song, but it sure was s-s-s-sad."

"Thanks, Junior," I said. "I can't tell you
how much it means to me that my last song has
gotten through to someone."

"Y-y-yeah, I'll b-b-bet."

"And the saddest part is that I'm an innocent
dog. I've been framed and railroaded and ac-

cused of terrible crimes I didn't commit, which means that this could be your last opportunity to . . . uh Junior, by any chance is your old man asleep?"

"W-w-w-well . . ."

"No he ain't." That was old man Wallace's hacksaw voice. "I heard the song. It wasn't sad, you ain't innocent, and even if you are it don't matter, because an innocent breakfast goes down just as good as one that's guilty."

Well, that was that. The sands of life were falling through the hour glass of time. Morning would come too soon for me.

12

BREAKFAST IS CANCELLED

I t was around first light that I noticed the wood down at the bottom of the door. It was kind of punky—not exactly rotten, but not firm either. It could be chewed. Given a little time, a guy just might chew himself a hole big enough to crawl through.

I wasn't sure I could chew my way out before Loper took me on that ride, but I didn't have anything better to do than to try. I started chewing and spitting, and by the time I heard people stirring down at the house, I had a hole big enough to squeeze through.

I stuck out my head and looked in all directions. The coast was clear. I slithered out and took a deep breath of fresh air. By George, I had done it! Once again, I had cheated the gravediggers and buzzards.

All at once the back door opened and Sally May walked out into the yard. I dropped down on my belly and didn't move. She called Little Alfred. When he didn't answer, she walked around to the side of the house. She looked this way and that, then her eyes fell on the yard gate. It was open.

Her jaw dropped and her hands went up to her face. Then she called for Loper, who was down at the corrals doing his morning chores. "The baby got out of the yard! He's out in the pasture! Hurry, we've got to find him before . . . !"

Loper dropped his feed bucket and came running to the house. Well, I was sure sorry to hear that my little pal Alfred had wandered off into the pasture, but whether he knew it or not, he was giving me a perfect opportunity to escape.

I glanced up at the two sleeping buzzards on the roof of the outhouse. "So long, suckers. I hate to miss that big breakfast, but I got places to go."

Wallace's head shot up. "What the . . . you git yourself right back in that jail house, Junior, you fell asleep and let our breakfast get away, you wake up right this minute!"

Junior's eyes popped open. "B-b-but Pa . . ."

"You see what you've done! It don't seem to matter how much I school you or how many sacrifices I make . . ."

I left the buzzards to fight it out. I turned my face to the north and headed out in a lope. I wasn't sure just yet where I would go, but I knew I had to put some empty space between me and the ranch—the ranch I had served so faithfully for so many years. I hated to leave, especially with false charges hanging over my memory, but Loper hadn't left me with too many choices.

I ran past the machine shed, past the mail box, across the county road, and took aim for that big caprock north of headquarters. I knew a secret trail I could take to the top, and once on top, I would have a straight shot to the high and lonesome.

Halfway up the caprock I stopped to catch my breath. I looked down at the broad valley below me while a fresh morning wind tugged at my ears. I was going to miss that place. I wondered what Drover was doing. The little dunce was probably sound asleep on his gunny sack, completely unaware that Little Alfred had wandered away and needed his help.

Off to the south I could see Sally May driving along the creek in the pickup. Loper was ahorseback, riding through some thick willows and calling Alfred's name. There was no sign of Drover. Or Alfred.

Well, that was too bad. I started up the last fifty feet of my climb to freedom. I hadn't gone more than three steps when I caught sight of something down below. I squinted at the spot and watched. There it was again: something small, two-legged, and diapered. Little Alfred.

"Hey, you people are looking down along the creek, but he's up here under the caprock!"

Well, that wasn't my problem. I started climbing again. Then I saw something else that made me stop. A horned cow came out of a draw. She looked at Little Alfred and bawled and shook her horns. The boy saw her and started toward her.

"Say, little buddy, you better stay away from that old sookie. She's got a new calf down there in those weeds and . . ."

That wasn't my problem. I had places to go. I started climbing again and forced myself not to look down again. I was pretty close to the top, just a few steps away from freedom, when I heard the scream.

I stopped.

Did I dare look down?

No! I had to run, I had to get off the ranch before . . .

Another scream. I looked down. The cow had charged. Little Alfred was on the ground screaming, and the cow was working him over with those horns.

There's a special bond between cowdogs and kids, don't you know, and no cowdog worthy of the name ever stood by and watched an innocent kid get mauled by a cow. The hair stood up on my back and I heard a deep growl come rumbling out of my throat.

By the time I got there, I had myself worked up into a fury. I went to her back side and started biting her on the heels. That's pretty risky. I mean, a guy can get his teeth rearranged if he's not careful, but I had to do something to take the cow's mind off Little Alfred.

She kicked at me, but I sank my teeth into her hocks. She bellered and whirled around and came after me with them horns. That's just what I wanted: me and her, one-on-one, nose-to-nose, in hand-to-hand combat.

I held back and dodged her hooks until she committed herself, then I rushed in and put my famous Australian fang lock on her nose. Brother, she didn't like that! She tossed her head and threw me around, but I held on. Finally she threw me off, but I was right back in the middle of her before she could get back to my little buddy.

I don't know how long this went on, but the next thing I knew, Sally May pulled up in the pickup and Loper was there on his horse. He took the double of his rope and laid it across the cow's back a couple of times, and I took a chunk out of her flank.

That was enough for her. She sold out and I barked her down the draw to her calf. If she hadn't had that calf to take care of, I just might have put a big hurt on her. She lucked out.

I trotted back and joined the others. Little Alfred had quit crying by then but he was still scared. Sally May and Loper checked him over to see how badly he was hurt. He had some bruises and a scratch or two, but otherwise he appeared to be all right.

Sally May set him down on the ground and when he saw me, he came right over and threw his arms around my neck. "Goggie! Goggie!" He derned near cut my wind off there for a minute, but at that point in my career, I figgered I could stand it. I gave the boy a big juicy lick in the face.

Out of the corner of my eye I could see Loper and Sally May watching us. Then a shadow passed over Loper's face. "What should I do about that dog? I had planned . . . well, you know,"

Sally May took a deep breath and shook her head. "Surely we were mistaken." *Right!* "Surely if we gave him one more chance, we wouldn't regret it." She came over and took my face in both her hands. "Hank, please leave my chickens alone."

I whapped my tail against the ground and swore a solemn oath: "Sally May, even though I'm completely innocent of the charges against me, I'll swear on my cowdog oath never to mess with your chickens again, even though I didn't do it the first time."

There. That covered it. We had us a deal. She even reached down and scratched me behind the ears. She drew back her hand, smelled of her fingers, and made a terrible face. "What does this dog *do* that makes him smell so bad! And look at my child, hugging his neck. It's a wonder that children survive."

Loper smiled. "They make a pair, don't they? Well, let's go to the house."

Little Alfred and I rode in the back of the pickup and Loper rode the horse back to the corrals. When we got to the place, Sally May went into the machine shed and gave me an extra coffee can of Co-op dog food. It wasn't all that great, but I ate every bite. Didn't want to hurt her feelings.

They went into the house and I drifted down to the gas tanks. As I predicted, Drover was curled up in a little white ball on his gunny sack. I woke him up.

"Wake up, son, the conquering hero has returned."

"What . . . who?" He looked at me with sleepy eyes, and one ear stuck up higher than the other one. "Oh, it's you. Gosh, Hank, I thought you were condemned."

I scratched around on my gunny sack and flopped down. "Nope. Cleared of all charges, found perfectly innocent, and decorated for extraordinary bravery in combat—all of that while you slept your life away."

"Gee, I guess I missed all the excitement."

"I guess you did, and it wasn't the first time."

"No, it was at least the second time."

"At least."

"Well, did you ever figure out who killed the chickens?"

I rolled over on my back and melted into the gunny sack. "I have suspicions, of course, but let's just say that in this instance, we're going to let sleeping dogs lie."

"What does that mean?"

"It means good night."

"Oh. Good night, Hank."

I heard his voice, but I had already slipped into some wonderful twitching dreams about Beulah the Collie and bones and chasing . . . rabbits.

G. L. Holmes